Marlon Finds a Way

A Twisty Tale of Anger, Trust & Friendship

Marlon

Silky

Marlon and Silky dedicate this book to all their fans and to Bennett, Julian, Louise and Helen. You inspire us every day!

Marlon Finds a Way

A Twisty Tale of Anger, Trust & Friendship

Story & Illustrations by
Dan Bailes

Cover Design by Erin McMahon

 Nice Dog Books / Washington, DC

Nice Dog Books

424 4th Street NE
Washington, DC 20002

 www.nicedogbooks.com

Publisher's Note: This is a work of fiction. Names, characters, places, and incidents are a product of the author's imagination. Locales and public names are sometimes used for atmospheric purposes. Any resemblance to actual people, living or dead, or to businesses, companies, events, institutions, or locales is completely coincidental.

Book design © 2017, BookDesignTemplates.com

Ordering Information: Special discounts are available on quantity purchases by libraries, schools, associations, and others. For details, contact the publisher at the address above.

Bailes / Dan. Author, Illustrator – First Edition

ISBN 978-1-953698-02-5

Library of Congress Control Number: 2021905170

Printed in the United States of America

Contents

Chapter 1

Marlon's Problem

"*Tell us a story,*" *said JJ.*

"*Yeah Mom, the one about the cat,*" *said Ben.*

"*Oh, you mean Mad Marlon?*" *said Mom.*

"*Yeah.*"

"Well, he was one mad cat."

"Why Mom?"

"Did someone make him mad? Like a dog?"

"Well, it wasn't a someone or a dog," said Mom. "It all started with a problem. At least, it was a problem for Marlon."

+ + +

Marlon isn't sure how the problem snuck up on him like a big sneeze (ah choo) or how it began to be a problem. Like a lot of problems, one day it's just there staring him in the face with a great big question mark.

Marlon takes a good look at his problem. Then the problem hops a few hops, cocks her head and plucks a fat little grub right out of the ground. She tilts back her head and swallows it whole.

Marlon blinks and sees his problem with new eyes. What he sees is a beautiful little sparrow named Silky. Marlon watches Silky hopping about, looking for bugs or seeds or crumbs left by JJ and Ben.

"Hey, that's us," said Ben.

"Yeah, we're in the story Mom," said JJ.

"Yes you are," said Mom.

+ + +

Silky stops and cocks her head. Her face and head are covered with feathers so soft they look like fur. Marlon blinks again but stays still. He doesn't want to scare her.

Silky looks around and spots a huge animal with sharp claws and big teeth. The animal doesn't move but she knows it's a cat. A cat! That's enough to scare any sparrow.

Silky takes a few hops, flaps her wings and flies off. Not too far, just far enough to land in a space where she feels safe with the other sparrows. Then she continues her search for food. Can't let that big scary cat get too close!

Chapter 2

The Creep and Pounce

Silky is just doing what birds do, but Marlon is not — and that is part of his problem. See, he knows exactly what he is "supposed" to do. He is supposed to squinch his eyes like two headlights and stare at Silky. He is supposed to watch every move she makes and slowly crouch down to make himself as small as possible. He is supposed to twitch his tail like a bee hunting a flower and start the creep and pounce.

"Yeah, he looks like a little tiger when he does that,"
JJ said.

"Creep and creep and creep and.........Pounce!" said
Ben, laughing.

"Cats are very good at doing the creep and
pounce. It's how they hunt," said Mom.

+ + +

You can try it sometime. If you are a cat, you already know
how...

You must move very slowly... carefully... and quietly... so
you can creep close to whatever you're stalking. You can't get
excited and wave your tail back and forth. You can't stop to
lick your paws or clean your face. You have to get very close
and keep still until the time is right. And then... POUNCE!

POUNCE so fast you can snatch it up before it even knows you're there.

"Sorry bird, you're about to be my lunch," said Ben.
"Oh, I don't like that," said JJ. "I don't like that cats go after birds."
"That's 'cause you're a birdbrain JJ."
"Am not! I just like cats _and_ birds."

+ + +

Well, birds don't like the creep and pounce. They don't like cats, either. Because birds know that cats just want to catch and eat them. Birds think cats are sneaky.

When sparrows sing to greet the day, they warn other birds to stay away... from cats:

> Can't trust a cat, that's where it's at
> If you want to get fat, don't play with a cat
> If you want to live long, a cat friend is wrong
> Cats are bad news, they give us the blues
> Can't trust a cat, that's where it's at

"Really, Mom?"

"Sure. What did you think they were singing about?"

Chapter 3

Mad Marlon

Marlon likes to practice the creep and pounce on his younger brother Albert. Marlon thinks it's funny. But Albert gets upset every time Marlon POUNCES him. Maybe that's why Marlon likes to do it.

"Does that sound like anyone I know?" said Mom.

"Ben and me," said JJ, "I'm like Albert and Ben is like Marlon."

+ + +

Every day while Albert is busy swatting some yarn or doing the hockey slim slam with a catnip mouse, Marlon gets ready to spring his big surprise. He creeps and gets really close. Albert is playing and doesn't see him. And...then... Marlon... POUNCES!

"Yowl!" "Mrowl!" They roll around on the carpet, fighting. Bodies locked together, they growl and howl, kick and bite. Hiss, scratch! "Mrowl" "Yowl!"

It sounds like a real cat fight but they're just playing. Marlon knows he should hold back. He's bigger, stronger and doesn't want to hurt his brother. He just likes surprising him and hearing him howl.

But sometimes Albert makes him mad, I mean really mad.

Like the time Albert grabbed the new catnip mouse before Marlon could play with it. Or the time Albert lapped up all the milk that JJ put out for both of them. Or when Ben gave Albert some of his pancake breakfast but forgot to give some to Marlon. Marlon became Mad Marlon then. He was so mad he did the scratch and bite.

Then Albert went "meew, meew" instead of "meow, meow" and ran away with his ears down and tail between his legs. Momma cat got mad and hissed at Marlon,

"No fighting, no biting!"
"He's your brother! You have to hold back!"
"Hold back, hold back!" Momma cat said.

Chapter 4

The Quiet Count and Check It Out

It's so unfair! It makes Marlon mad. He doesn't want to hold back. He doesn't want Momma cat to hiss at him. "Mrowl!"

What he does want is to have fun and do whatever he feels like doing. "Mrowl!" Marlon walks away and sits in the corner, licking his paws.

He looks up and spots Albert playing with the catnip mouse. Marlon waits for a bit, then decides to do the creep and pounce. They tussle and scuffle, romp and wrestle. Then something happens, a poke or a kick. Marlon gets mad and does the scratch and bite. Then Momma cat hisses at him.

That's how he became Mad Marlon.

He doesn't like being Mad Marlon. But now everyone calls him that. And every day is the same: creep and pounce, play fight, real fight, hissing Momma cat and he turns into Mad Marlon all over again.

One day he says to Momma cat. "I don't want to be Mad Marlon. I just want to be regular old Marlon like before."

"Okay," Momma cat says, "I can show you how to make a change." Marlon's whiskers twitch and his ears perk up, ready to listen.

She says, "Use the Quiet Count to help you put aside the mad feelings. Then you won't get so angry and do the scratch and bite. And then I won't get mad and hiss at you."

Here's what she tells him: "When you feel yourself getting angry or feel the mad building up inside you, just stop what you're doing and do the Quiet Count."

"The Quiet Count?" said JJ.

"That's right," Mom said, "just stop and count quietly to yourself."

"Counting is easy, Mom."

"Yes, counting is the easy part."

"You should do that Ben," JJ said. "You're always banging on me."

"You too," Ben said. "Before you take my stuff or play with my toys. You should count and remember to leave them alone."

"Mom, if counting is the easy part, what's the hard part?"

"The hard part is doing it before you get really mad or before the mad takes over."

"What do you mean, Mom?"

"With you boys," said Mom, "it's before you grit your teeth or your hand turns into a fist or your tummy feels like it's on fire. Those are signs you're getting mad and it's time to do the Quiet Count."

+ + +

15

Marlon tries to remember to use the Quiet Count. He tries to slowly count to 10 whenever he feels angry. When he uses the Quiet Count, he can feel the anger walking away. That's right, the anger just says, "oh, never mind" and slowly drifts away. I guess that's why you have to take your time when you count, to give anger a chance to say goodbye and leave.

"Cats counting? Come on mom!"

"Yes, of course cats can count," said Mom. "Just because you can't hear them do it doesn't mean they don't know how. Cats are smart. Believe me."

+ + +

Most of the time doing the Quiet Count works. But sometimes it doesn't make the anger go away. That's when Marlon tries the Check It Out.

The Check It Out kind of goes like this: Marlon says to himself, "I'm a big cat now. I have a choice about what I do. Yes, I'm mad but I can use my words. I can use my words to check it out, check it out, check it out." That's how Momma cat explains it to him.

"Cats can't talk, Mom," said JJ.

"Yeah. I've never heard Albert or Marlon say people words," said Ben.

"They're cat words, silly, not people words," said Mom. "You know cats have their own language. Well, what are they telling you when they purr? I'm happy? I love you? I feel good?"

Mom smiled. "Cats purr to tell us something nice in cat language. They don't purr when they're angry. They hiss and growl when they're mad."

+ + +

Still, Marlon doesn't always do the Quiet Count or the Check It Out. Because sometimes he just forgets. And other times the mad takes over and he can't make himself stop in time to do it. And sometimes... well he is just a cat, after all. And cats behave like cats. Except when a cat like Marlon wants to make friends with a sparrow. That's a whole different ball game.

Chapter 5

Marlon's Silky

Marlon really, really likes Silky. Yes, Silky is just a little bird. And all cats know that little birds like Silky are just something to chase, catch and eat for breakfast. But not for Marlon. No way! And, that is his problem.

He doesn't want to chase, catch or eat Silky.

Marlon thinks Silky is beautiful. Yes, beautiful with her soft downy face, little fluffy gray body and powerful brown and black striped wings. That's what he sees when she stands still. But most of the time she is a blur as she hops about the yard or flies into the trees. It's hard to get a good look at her. And you know what else? Silky can fly really fast. Really fast when she wants to.

Marlon wishes he could do what Silky can do.

No, silly goose, I don't mean eat grubs or bugs. Thinking about eating bugs or grubs makes Marlon shiver all the way from his paws to his whiskers. No bugs. No grubs.

"Me too. No grubs and bugs," said Ben.
"You're a Grubby Buggy," JJ said, poking Ben.
Ben gave JJ a look.
"Give me a hug, my little bugs," said Mom.

+ + +

What Marlon wants to do that Silky can do is this — he wants to fly. He sees that Silky can fly anywhere she chooses. Watching Silky, he thinks she can do all these cool things. I don't want to do the creep and pounce and eat her. No way.

My cat brain says, "Do it." But there's also a little voice inside me that says, "Don't do it!" Then it says, "Find another way."

See, all the other cats see a sparrow like Silky in just one way: bite-sized. Silky is definitely that. That's what Albert says to Marlon, "Silky is bite-sized - a big yum."

But Marlon thinks, "Silky is so pretty, I love watching her. I don't want to eat her. Maybe we can be friends. But how?"

Chapter 6

Silky's Silky

Silky is a house sparrow. She's a smart bird. She knows that Marlon is prowling around her favorite pecking grounds. He's a cat and that's bad news. Where cats and birds are concerned, cats are trouble on the double.

Like all house sparrows, Silky loves to be around people. Because people like JJ and Ben often drop little bits of food when they roam around outside. Silky loves to find those delicious crumbs and eat them. People leave little goodies lying around for nests, too – like string, paper, straw and little strips of plastic. She can use those!

Plus, people-houses have all kinds of little secret places that are perfect for hide-away nests. They're tucked away up high and safe from curious creatures. And hard for a cat to reach. "People-perfect places," Silky calls them. (Try saying that several times in a row!)

Every morning Silky likes to chirp to greet the day. "Chirp, chirp" – another great day to fly around. "Chirp, chirp" – another lovely morning for singing. "Chirp, chirp" – such yummy crumbs and bits of bread to eat. "Chirp, chirp" – how are you? Nice to see you. "Chirp" – I'm glad there aren't any cats who prowl around here.

[Oh, she can't chirp that one any more.]

So now, after chirping, she has to keep one eye open for food and one eye open for Marlon. That makes her a little cross-eyed. Sigh. And when she does see him, (she doesn't usually hear him because he moves so quietly) she scoots away really fast. I mean really fast.

One minute she's there searching for crumbs or bugs. The next minute, poof, she's gone.

Chapter 7

Marlon Makes a Plan

So now do you understand Marlon's problem? He keeps thinking about it. He's supposed to be a certain way - everyone tells him that. And act a certain way. Everyone says, "you are a cat. Be a cat." And, "Silky is for the birds!" And then they laugh.

That's no help. Is Marlon supposed to "act like a cat" and be sneaky and tricky and catch as many birds like Silky as he can? And eat them up? No way!

Marlon sighs, thinking, "So, what should I do? I think Silky is such a dazzling darter. I just want to be friends, not eat her."

Marlon paces back and forth, tail twitching. He stops and looks at the sky. Marlon sees some pretty clouds but they don't help. He paces back and forth. He stops and looks at the ground. He sees a nice big pile of red and gold leaves that Ben and JJ raked this morning.

His tail twitches some more. He starts to pace again and stops. Marlon has an idea. He looks up at the sky and meows, "I know what to do. I'll try to fly!"

Here is Marlon's idea:

"If I can fly, then Silky won't think of me as a cat. When she sees me fly, she'll think of me more like a bird. Yes! If I'm more like her, then maybe she will like me and not fly away. Maybe she will stick around and we can play and become friends."

28

Marlon smiles. (Yes, just like us, cats can smile when they feel happy). Marlon thinks, "I hope it will work, I just need to make a plan."

Marlon begins to sing:

Oh, I feel so grand
I just need a plan
To float through the air
No worry or care
I'll have so much fun
Fly up to the sun
And then I will land
In leaves or the sand

And Silky will say
Come on and let's play
Today is the day
When we fly away
And no one will say
That this story ends
And you can't be friends.
No, you can't be friends.

Chapter 8

Marlon Tries to Fly

Marlon curls up to think about a plan. As he thinks about it, he has questions: "How can I fly? I don't have wings. I can't just hop up and fly like Silky. Hmmm. Maybe I can climb up something that is really tall. Taller than a house. Maybe a tree will work. This sounds like a plan: climb up a tree for a head start and then jump off and fly!"

Here's what happens:

Marlon looks up at the maple tree where Silky likes to sing with her sparrow friends. The tree is tall. Marlon is small. He thinks, "I really like having my paws here on the ground. But if I want Silky to like me and be my friend, I've got to be more like her."

He looks up at the tree once again. It's still tall. So tall. He squares his shoulders and takes a deep breath, "Okay. Let's do this."

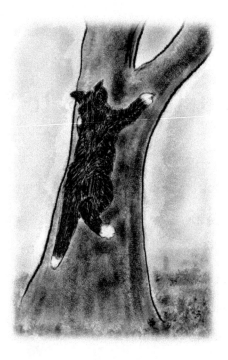

Marlon jumps onto the trunk and uses his sharp claws to slowly climb up the tree. He climbs higher, passing branch over branch. Many of the leaves have fallen and he can see bright colors in the ones that remain. He looks past the leaves and sees some puffy clouds in the sky and the roofs of nearby houses.

He looks down and sees the pile of red, orange and yellow leaves that Ben and JJ raked. Down there, that pile of leaves looks pretty small. "Hmmm," he says, "I must be pretty high up. Okay, time to fly. I hope you're watching me, Silky."

Marlon looks up at the clouds one more time, spreads his paws as wide as he can and gets ready. Still holding on, he thinks, "When I fly I will just float around in the air like one of those clouds. Maybe even go high enough to touch one. Okay, nice and easy does it."

Marlon lets go.

He's going down. Fast. Oh no! Air whooshes by his face. He looks down. He turns and twists to stay upright. The ground rushes up at him. Whoomp!

He lands deep in the pile of leaves.

"Oh, thank you leaves," Marlon says, once he gets his breath back. "I'm so happy you were there to see me fly."

Marlon gets up. His legs are a little wobbly. He takes a few shaky steps and sits. He picks some leaves from his fur and gives himself a big shake. "Well, that was really quick," he says. "I can fly down really fast. But how do I fly up?"

Marlon gives another shake and looks at the clouds high above the tree. "Well, maybe I should try again," he says. "This time I'll go higher."

Chapter 9

Marlon Tries Again

Marlon goes back to the maple tree and climbs up the trunk, passing branch by branch until he's higher than before. He sees the clouds and smiles. "Look out clouds, I'm coming to chase you!"

He takes a deep breath and steps off the branch. Once again, he goes down. Really fast. Before he can flap his legs and paws, the ground rushes up at him. Whoomp! He lands deep in the pile of leaves.

He tries to stand but his legs say, "Sit!" He blinks his eyes and looks around. What happened? Marlon is so confused, "I want to go up to the clouds. It's not fair! My flying gets all mixed up." He lets out a big sigh, "It looks so easy when Silky does it. I must be doing something wrong."

"He's falling, not flying," said JJ.
"Yeah. I guess he's not so smart," said Ben.
"He is too. Marlon's a good cat!"
"Well, maybe he never learned about gravity."
"He's just a cat. Gravity is a people thing."
"No, gravity is for animals too. It's like a law."
"Well, if he's going to jump out of a tree, it's a good thing he's a cat.
"Why?"
"Cause cats have nine lives."

+ + +

Marlon steps out of the leaf pile. He takes a deep breath and gives a big shake from his head to his tail. He says, "Okay, one more time. Come on legs, we can do this. Think up, up, up!"

Again, Marlon goes back to the tree and climbs as high as he can go. He looks around. It's cool and quiet. It feels nice to be so high up. "Hello clouds, here I come."

"Okay." Marlon stretches like he's going to do the POUNCE. "Remember, up, up, up." He leaps as high as he can into the air.

Well, you know what happens. Right! The ground rushes up at him and Whoomp! He lands deep in the pile of leaves. So deep you can't even see him.

Nothing moves for a while and then the leaves rustle and Marlon's head pokes out of the leaf pile. He blinks his eyes and looks around. Slowly, he pulls himself up and out of the pile. And very carefully, he plops down. His head droops, his shoulders droop. Even his whiskers droop. Finally, he stands up and wobbles on his wobbly legs.

"Oh, no," Marlon sighs. "I want to fly up high in the sky. How come I only fly down?" He shakes his head and starts to sing:

> *Oh me, oh my*
> *I try and try*
> *Can't reach the sky*
> *I don't know why*
> *I want to cry*
> *I just can't fly*
> *Oh me, oh my*
> *Why can't I fly*

Marlon hears chirping, lots of chirping. He looks up at a maple tree. It's Silky and her sparrow friends. They're flapping their wings and chirping. "Chirp, Chirp."

"What happened to your wings? Oh, right, you don't have any," Silky chirps. "Everyone knows birds have wings. Nice trying, but no wings, no flying. Here's the last word – I guess you're not a bird."

Chapter 10

Cats Can't Fly

Marlon is mad. "They're making fun of me!" he hisses.

He wants to leap and POUNCE, scratch and bite. He gives a low growl, crouches down and gets ready. And then he remembers, first do the Quiet Count.

He growls and starts an angry count, "One, two, three..." He remembers he likes Silky. "Four, five, six..." He remembers he wants her to like him. "Seven, eight, nine…" He remembers that scratching, kicking and biting will not make her like him. "Ten…"

Marlon sighs. Counting helps, but he's still mad. Mad that he can only fly down, mad that Silky is making fun of him. Maybe even mad that he's a cat and not a bird.

Marlon is just about to hiss "I hate you" and pounce on Silky, but something makes him stop. He thinks of Momma cat and how she likes to say, "if you don't know for sure, use your words. Ask a question and check it out, check it out."

Marlon takes a deep breath, looks up at Silky and asks, "Are you making fun of me?"

"Maybe a little," Silky says, giving a chirp that sounds more like a laugh, if sparrows could laugh. "But what I said is true. If you don't have wings, you can't fly."

"Don't be dense, it's common sense!" chirp her sparrow friends. "It's simple, why? No wings, no fly!"

Silky looks right at Marlon.

"We're birds. Our bodies are very light and just the right shape for flying. Our bones and feathers are very light too."

She flaps her wings, lifts up and settles on another branch.

"We have strong muscles so we can flap our wings really fast. And see how our wings look? They're perfect for catching the air and lifting us up."

She flies up in the air and the other sparrows follow her. Marlon lifts a paw and looks at it.

He sighs and looks up at the sky. "Well, I'm strong too," he thinks, "but I don't have feathers or wings. I may really want to fly, but my body can't do it." He looks up at Silky and down at his paws. "I guess she's just telling me the truth."

Marlon gets up and stretches. "Well, at least one thing worked. I used my words and checked it out. And now I don't feel mad anymore."

As he slowly makes his way back home, his legs feel very stiff and sore. "I guess I need to try something else," he says, looking back at Silky and the sparrows as they fly down to the ground for their next meal.

Chapter 11

High Chirpy Voices

Back at home, Marlon curls up and takes a nap. While he sleeps, he has a lovely dream. In his dream, he's up in the maple tree. He sees Silky and her sparrow friends singing to greet the morning. He loves their high, chirpy voices. Their song is so sweet, it makes him feel good.

He wakes, stretches and sits up. He has an idea: maybe I can try to sing like Silky and the sparrows. Hey, that sounds like a rock band.

This is Marlon's new plan:

"Silky likes to sing. Maybe if I sing with a nice chirpy voice she will think, he can't be a bad cat if he sings like me. He must be okay. Then maybe she will stick around and we can sing together and be friends."

Marlon runs through the cat door and trots outside. He sits up tall, opens his mouth and begins to sing. But he doesn't chirp like Silky. What comes out of his mouth sounds more like a cat calling for a friend, but in cat language. "Mrowl, eyoowwll," is what he sings to the world.

JJ pokes his head out the door. "What's that sound?"

"Marlon, are you sick?" Ben says, following JJ outside.

Marlon tries to sing again, "Owwwllyooo."

"It sounds like a very sick cat!" JJ says, trying to see where the strange yowl-y noise is coming from.

"Rowwlloorr."

"Sounds like a sad tired ghost."

"Or a little kitty cat that missed his supper."

"Come on Marlon. No more howl-y yowl-y. It's not Halloween, you know."

JJ looks around the yard and spots Marlon. "Come here little kitty, we'll give you some milk."

Marlon likes the sound of milk. He walks over and rubs his body against JJ's legs. "Mmrowll."

"You sound like a sick puppy."

Silky and the sparrows don't say anything. They watch as Marlon follows Ben and JJ inside to get some milk.

Marlon laps up the milk, stretches and lies down. He puts his head down and looks at the floor. "I guess singing isn't going to work. Well, I can't fly and can't chirp... I guess I need to try something else." He gives a long sigh and closes his eyes.

Chapter 12

What Can He Do?

Marlon thinks about Silky and the sparrows. They're really different from me. I have fur, they have feathers. They have two feet, I have four paws. They have a beak and peck, I have a mouth with sharp teeth and bite. Hmmm... do we have anything that's the same?

He says to himself, "Okay, I'm not a bird and I can't pretend to be one. And anyway, Silky knows I'm not a bird. So, I should stop trying to be something I'm not and just be me, Marlon."

Marlon starts to pace in a big circle. Pacing helps him think.

"Walking helps me think," said Ben.
"That's because you're a bird brain," said JJ.
"That makes no sense."
"You're so dense. Go sit on a fence."

+ + +

Marlon wonders how to show Silky that he likes her. He asks himself some questions.

"What do I like that Silky might like? Or, what can I give her to show her I want to be friends. Hmm. I see people give each other things all the time. JJ and Ben's mom gives them food. Ben and JJ give me food. Maybe I can give her food. Hmm. It should be something nice."

He thinks some more, "I can catch a mouse and give it to her. I gave one to Ben and JJ the other day. But they just said 'eeww' and threw it in the garbage. I don't know why they did that, it was a perfectly good mouse."

"I remember that," said JJ. "I felt sad for the little mouse."

"Me too," said Ben.

+ + +

"I can't give her a grub or bug," Marlon thinks. "I don't even know how to catch one. And they're too yucky. We like to eat different things, so food won't work."

Then Marlon has an interesting thought, "Hmmm. JJ and Ben give me things to play with. I love that catnip mouse they gave me. And that yarn ball they got from their mom. I love yarn balls. They're so fun to bat around and chase."

"Maybe Silky will like that. I'll give her some yarn. Maybe she can use it for something. There's some red yarn in the big room. I'll go get some."

"I love that red and blue sweater you made for me, Mom," said Ben.

"Me too," said JJ, "it's really warm."

+ + +

So, Marlon takes a nice piece of yarn in his mouth and goes outside. He looks around and hears some chirps. "I always know where to find her," he thinks. "All I have to do is listen."

Then he sees Silky taking a dust bath. She wiggles her body in the dirt and scoops up a cloud of dust with her wings.

"What's a dust bath?"

"You boys take baths with water," Mom said. "Well, sparrows and other birds like taking a bath with dirt.

"Dirt? Sounds yucky!"

"Well, the dirt keeps their feathers from getting greasy or stuck together. I know it sounds funny, but the dust helps keep their feathers clean and dry. So, it's easy to fly."

"You made a rhyme, Mom."

"Hush boys, stop the noise."

+ + +

Silky sees Marlon's shadow moving towards her. She takes a quick hop and flies up to a branch on the big maple tree.

Marlon stops and looks up at her. He gives a little meow and shakes his head. He puts the yarn down and walks away from it so Silky can get it. "This is for you, Silky. I just want to be friends," he says.

51

Chapter 13

Trust

Silky looks down at the yarn and looks at Marlon. "You're a cat. Everyone knows cats are trouble on the double."

"What do you mean?"

"You're a cat and cats think birds are just a big yum."

Silky spreads her wings and lifts up to the next branch. "You can't just say you want to be my friend. You have to show me."

No one has ever said that to Marlon before. "But I got this piece of yarn for you. I really like you and thought you would like it."

"I do like yarn. I can use it for my nest. But maybe you're trying to trick me. Anyway, your words are not enough. I don't trust you."

Now Marlon is confused. He rubs his whiskers with his paws and tries to think.

Momma cat always says, "use your words, ask a question and check it out." But Silky says words aren't enough. Momma cat says words, Silky says no.

This makes Marlon angry. How can they both be right?

Just thinking about it makes Marlon even madder. He's so mad he almost leaps up the tree to POUNCE on Silky. But something stops him. It's like a little voice inside him is saying, "If I POUNCE then I will scare her and she really won't trust me. I better find another way."

He slowly counts to ten and tries again. Think, Marlon, think. He decides to check it out with a question, so he asks, "Why do you say words are not enough?"

Silky looks at him for a moment. She cocks her head and says, "Because actions speak louder than words. What you <u>do</u> is really important. More important than what you say."

"Oh," Marlon says. "Look, the yarn is a gift. That's all. I don't want to hurt you."

Silky just chirps, waiting.

Chapter 14

Actions

Marlon thinks, "If actions speak louder than words, I have to do something. How can I show her I just want to be friends?" Then he has an idea.

Marlon says, "We'll do something together. Let's play a game and I'll show you that you can trust me."

Silky looks back at him. Should she give him a chance? She looks at her sparrow friends in the tree. They start chirping at once,

"Can't trust a cat and that's a fact!"
"Better pause and watch those claws!"
"Don't be a fool, he's after you!"
"Keep eyes on him and stay on a limb!"
"That cat plays dumb but you're his big yum!"
"Silky, if you do it, you'll boohoo it!"

But Silky is curious. Maybe this cat Marlon is not like the other cats. Maybe it will be a good thing. She can take a chance and see how it goes. Anyway, she can fly away really fast if it looks like he's going to do the creep and pounce. So, she says, "Ok."

Silky flies down from the tree, hops a few hops toward Marlon and stops. She looks hard at him. Marlon twitches his nose and gives her a small cat smile but doesn't move. He even keeps his tail flat on the ground. He stays still.

Silky starts to peck the ground.

She pecks hard and keeps one eye on Marlon. She pecks again and each peck makes a little thump sound. She pecks out a rhythm that goes like this: thump de thump, thump de thump, thump de thump.

Marlon listens to Silky's pecking and then starts to hiss along with the beat. It sounds like this: thump de hiss, thump de hiss, thump de hiss, thump de hiss.

Marlon uses his mad voice to make the hiss sound, but he isn't mad. He just likes the way it sounds with Silky's thumps. And Silky does, too.

Then Marlon changes the rhythm like this: thump de thump de hiss, thump de thump de hiss, thump de thump de hiss, thump de thump de hiss.

Silky starts to chirp. She goes chirp de chirp, chirp de chirp, chirp de chirp. Marlon takes out his claws. Silky stops, nervous.

"No, Silky," Marlon says, "I'm just going to use them for our beats. Keep going."

So, Silky does and this is how it sounds now: chirp de chirp scratch, chirp de chirp scratch, chirp de chirp scratch, chirp de chirp scratch.

It sounds good and they spend some time putting together beats with different sounds and different rhythms. They can do all that by just using their bodies and voices.

"I like that we can do something together," says Silky. "That makes me feel better about you being a cat." Then, she picks up the yarn in her beak. "This will look great in my nest. Thank you!"

Marlon just smiles. He can see Silky is starting to trust him. Marlon thinks they can spend time together as long as Silky feels safe from his sharp claws and fierce teeth. So, Marlon never does the crouch and pounce around her - even in play.

After they do their beats together, Silky knows that she can trust Marlon. And Marlon gets to spend some time with Silky, just like he wants.

Pretty soon they become good friends.

Thinking about how it all worked out, Marlon feels good about doing the Quiet Count and the Check it Out. When he gets mad, he tries to remember to use them. Silky sees him trying and she likes that. And he feels proud that he can do it. It makes him feel like one cool cat.

Marlon never learns to fly... and he still doesn't like to eat grubs or bugs. Yes, he tries some once and says they taste like dirt and smelly socks. And Silky never makes fun of Marlon again.

Marlon and Silky still do beats together. And every day about this time, they get together to lay down some new sounds. The other birds and little animals sometimes come to listen.

And tell you what, if you're very quiet when you walk in the forest, you might be able to hear them too.

"I like that story, Mom," said JJ.

"Let's go out and see if we can hear them," said Ben.

"Let me know if you do," said Mom. "And have fun you two."

+ + +

Thanks for Reading

Thanks for reading our story and I hope you enjoyed it. Here's a Q&A about how I came to write *Marlon Finds a Way*.

Dan, why did you write this story?

I watched my daughter teach her boys the "Quiet Count" and "Check it Out" to help them manage their feelings of frustration and anger. I thought, wow, there's something really useful in all that. Maybe I could write a story about it.

Any other themes in the story?

Well, I was curious about how we often only see things from our point of view. Well, that's not a good way to make friends. And I think empathy is so important. It helps us see the world through another person's eyes.

Why a bird and cat?

I liked starting with two creatures who would never be comfortable with each other and see what might happen when one wants to make friends with the other. How would they move from suspicion to trust?

What would you like people to take away from the story?

I'd be thrilled if my story helps kids realize that we're all special in our own way. And to appreciate what each of us has to offer. Don't get discouraged or give up when something seems difficult. Just give it your best effort and be proud that you did.

Anything else?

I hope you'll take a moment and leave a review. I read all the reviews and comments because they help me become a better writer. And reviews help other people decide if they want to read the story, too. So please leave a review and let me know what you think. And thanks! It's a big help and I really appreciate it.

You can find other books you may like at www.NiceDogBooks.com. And be sure to check out *Emmalene A Tiger's Tale*, a funny feline frolic I'm sure you'll enjoy.

Dan and Kukka

Acknowledgments

I'd like to thank the following people for reading and commenting on early drafts of this book. It's so helpful to have another person's eye looking over the material and offering their feedback. Marlon's quest for Silky's friendship wouldn't be nearly as coherent without your help! So, a great big thank you to Alyson Shade, Hope Hazen, Melissa Mial, Kathleen MacDonald, Elizabeth Brionez, Pearl Bailes and Sharon Ferguson, my touchstone and partner in crime. Thank you so much!

About The Author

Dan writes funny chapter books for children and everyone who likes a good story. His tales feature animals and siblings who may bicker, but then come together to solve a problem or meet a challenge. His quirky characters can charm us with their silly delights or surprising insights. And it's fun to watch them develop self-reliance, grit and the courage to make a change.

He wrote his first stories when his daughter and son were young and is excited that he can continue the tradition for his grandchildren Bennett, Julian, Louise and Helen. With whimsical humor and a playful imagination, Dan's stories are often inspired by something they shared or an issue they were trying to deal with.

Dan lives in Washington, DC with his wife Sharon and their dog, KukkaTahti. When he's not writing or reading or thinking silly thoughts, he likes to hang out with Sharon, play with Kukka, do yoga, take pictures, listen to music or just take a deep breath and watch the flowers grow.